FOR MY GRANDCHILDREN
AND TO ALL THE CHILDREN
OF NIGERIA

—CHINUA ACHEBE

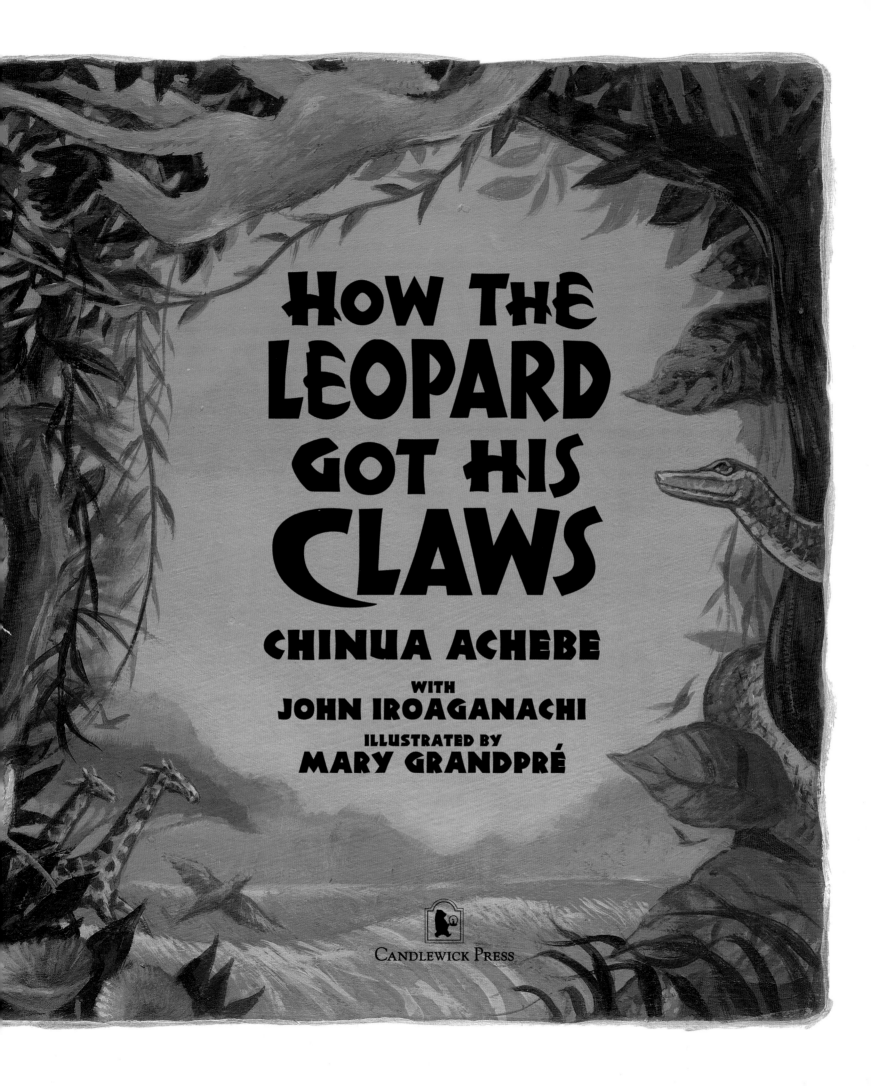

How the Leopard Got His Claws

Chinua Achebe

with
John Iroaganachi

ILLUSTRATED BY
Mary Grandpré

Candlewick Press

In the beginning . . .

all the animals in the forest lived as friends. Their king was the leopard. He was strong, but gentle and wise. He ruled the animals well, and they all liked him.

At that time, the animals did not fight one another. Most of them had no sharp teeth or claws. They did not need them. Even King Leopard had only small teeth.

He had no claws at all.

Only the dog had big, sharp teeth. The other animals said he was ugly, and they laughed at him.

"It is foolish to carry sharp things in the mouth," said the tortoise.

"I think so, too," said the goat.

The monkey jumped in and began to tease the dog.

"Don't worry, my dear friend," said the monkey. "You need your teeth to clear the land on your farm."

The animals laughed at the monkey's joke.

When the farming season came around, King Leopard led the animals to their farmland. They all worked hard to prepare their plots. At the end of the day, they returned home tired. As they rested, they told stories and drank palm wine.

But soon it would be the rainy season, and the animals would have no shelter from the rain. The deer took this problem to King Leopard. They talked about it for a long time. King Leopard decided to call the animals together to discuss it.

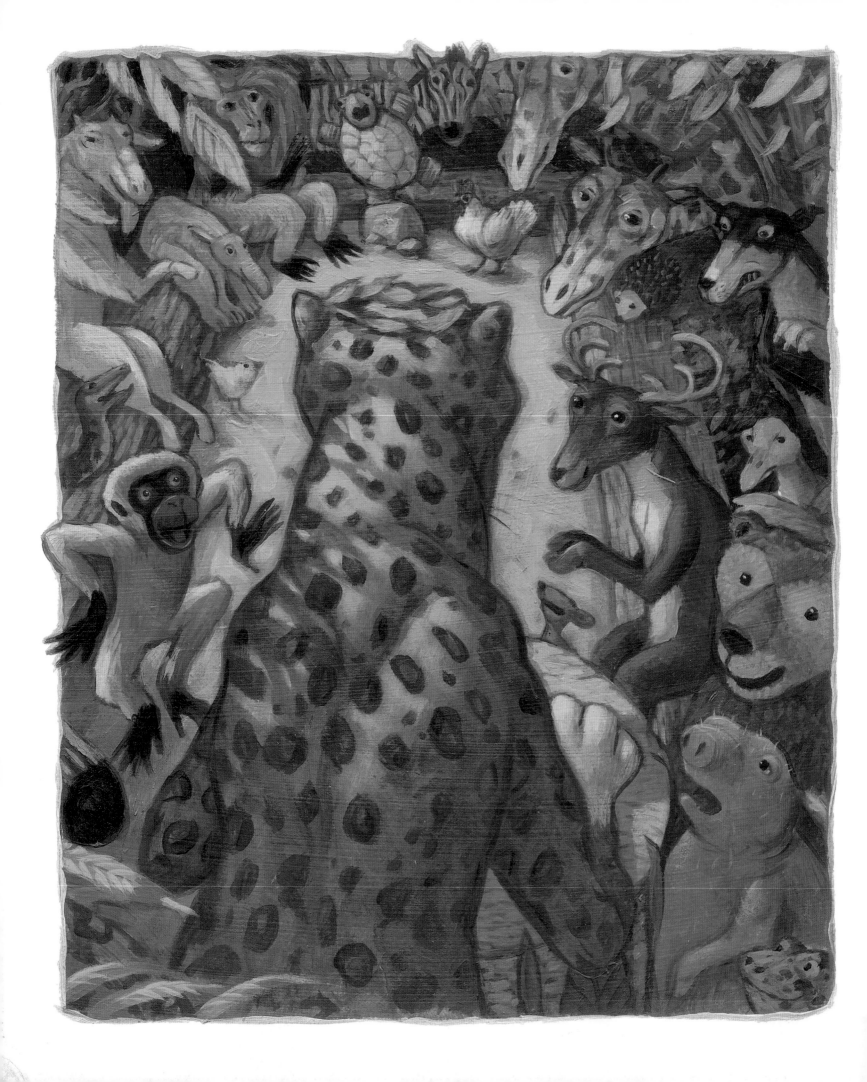

One bright morning, King Leopard beat his royal drum. When the animals heard the drum, they gathered at the village square. The tortoise was there. The goat was there, too. The sheep, the grasscutter, the monkey, the hedgehog, the baboon, the dog, and many others were there.

King Leopard greeted them and said, "I have called you together to plan how we can make ourselves a common shelter."

"This is a good idea," said the giraffe.

"Yes, a very good idea," said many other animals.

"But why do we need a common house?" asked the dog.

He had never liked King Leopard.

"The dog has asked a good question," said the duck. "Why do we need a common shelter?"

"We do need somewhere to rest when we return from our farms," replied King Leopard.

"And besides," said the goat, "we need a shelter from the rain."

"I don't mind being wet," said the duck. "In fact, I like it. I know the goat does not like water on his body. Let him go and build a shelter."

"We need a shelter," said the monkey, jumping up and down in excitement.

"Perhaps we need one. Perhaps we don't," said the lazy baboon, sitting on the low fence of the square.

The dog spoke again. "We are wasting our time. Those who need a shelter should build it. I live in a cave, and it is enough for me." Then he walked away. The duck followed him out.

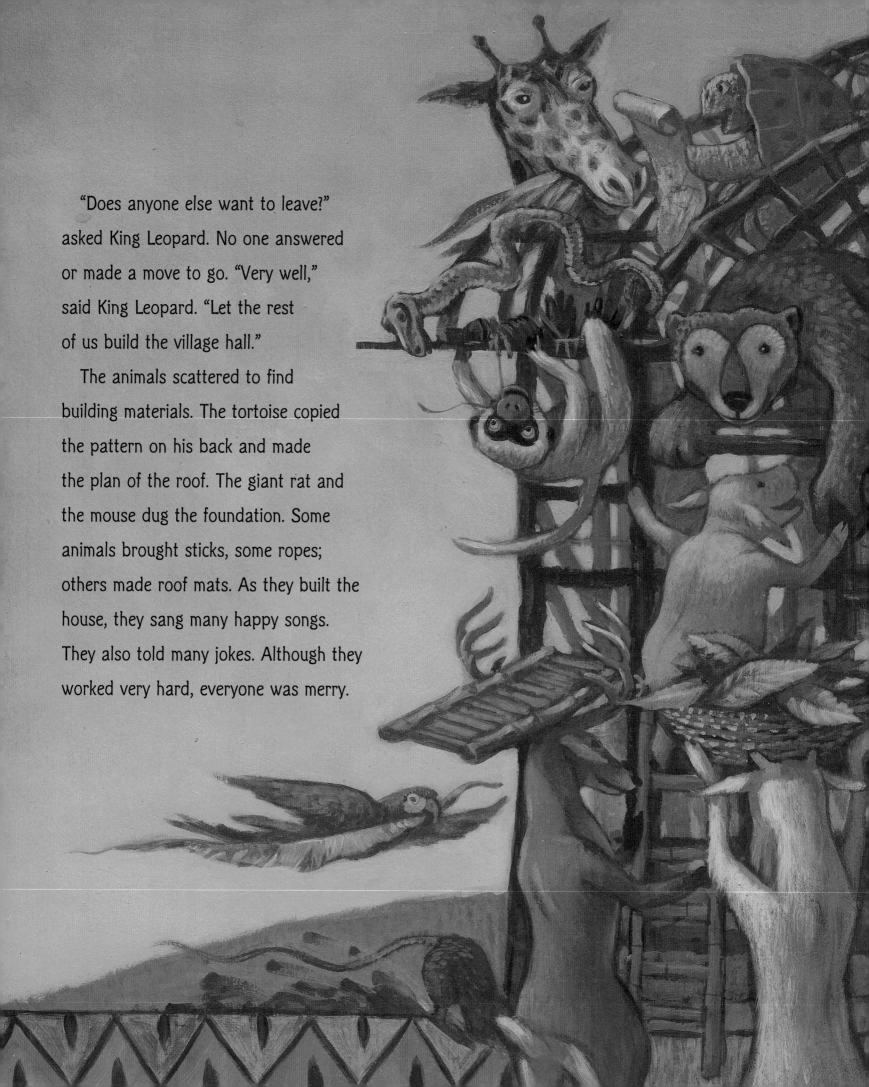

"Does anyone else want to leave?" asked King Leopard. No one answered or made a move to go. "Very well," said King Leopard. "Let the rest of us build the village hall."

The animals scattered to find building materials. The tortoise copied the pattern on his back and made the plan of the roof. The giant rat and the mouse dug the foundation. Some animals brought sticks, some ropes; others made roof mats. As they built the house, they sang many happy songs. They also told many jokes. Although they worked very hard, everyone was merry.

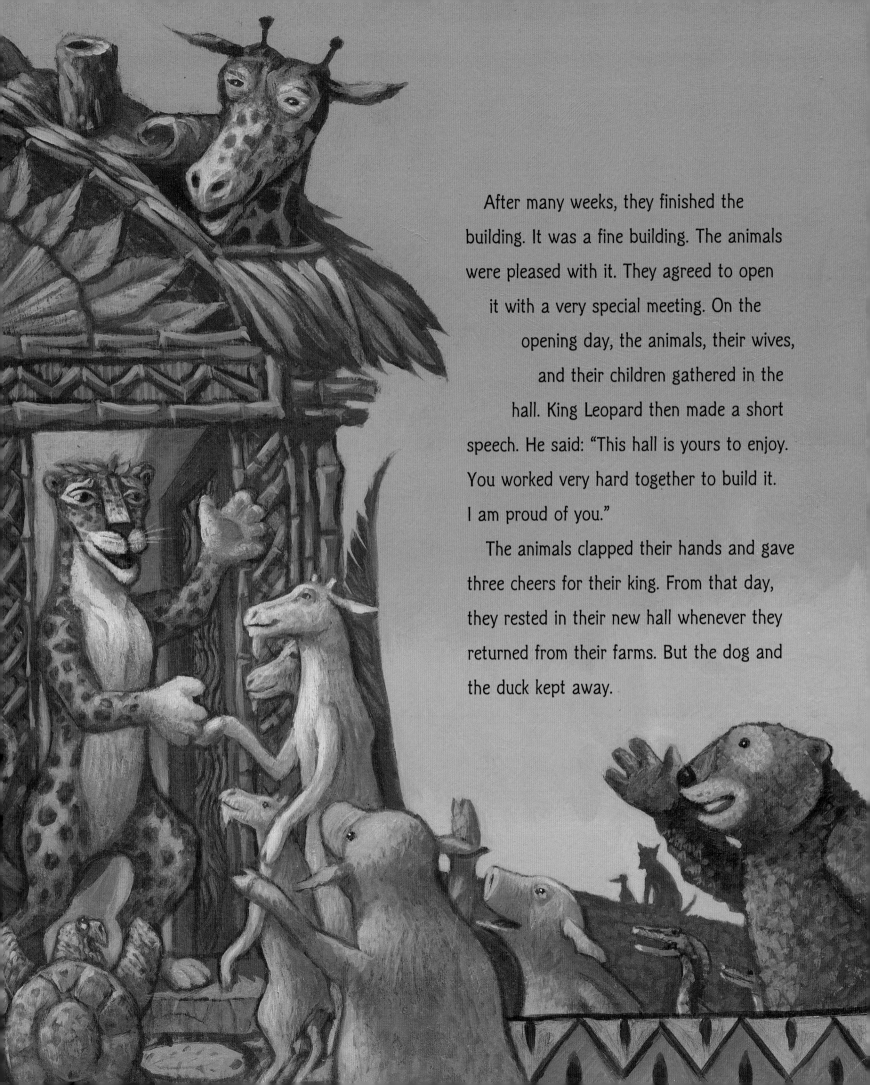

After many weeks, they finished the building. It was a fine building. The animals were pleased with it. They agreed to open it with a very special meeting. On the opening day, the animals, their wives, and their children gathered in the hall. King Leopard then made a short speech. He said: "This hall is yours to enjoy. You worked very hard together to build it. I am proud of you."

The animals clapped their hands and gave three cheers for their king. From that day, they rested in their new hall whenever they returned from their farms. But the dog and the duck kept away.

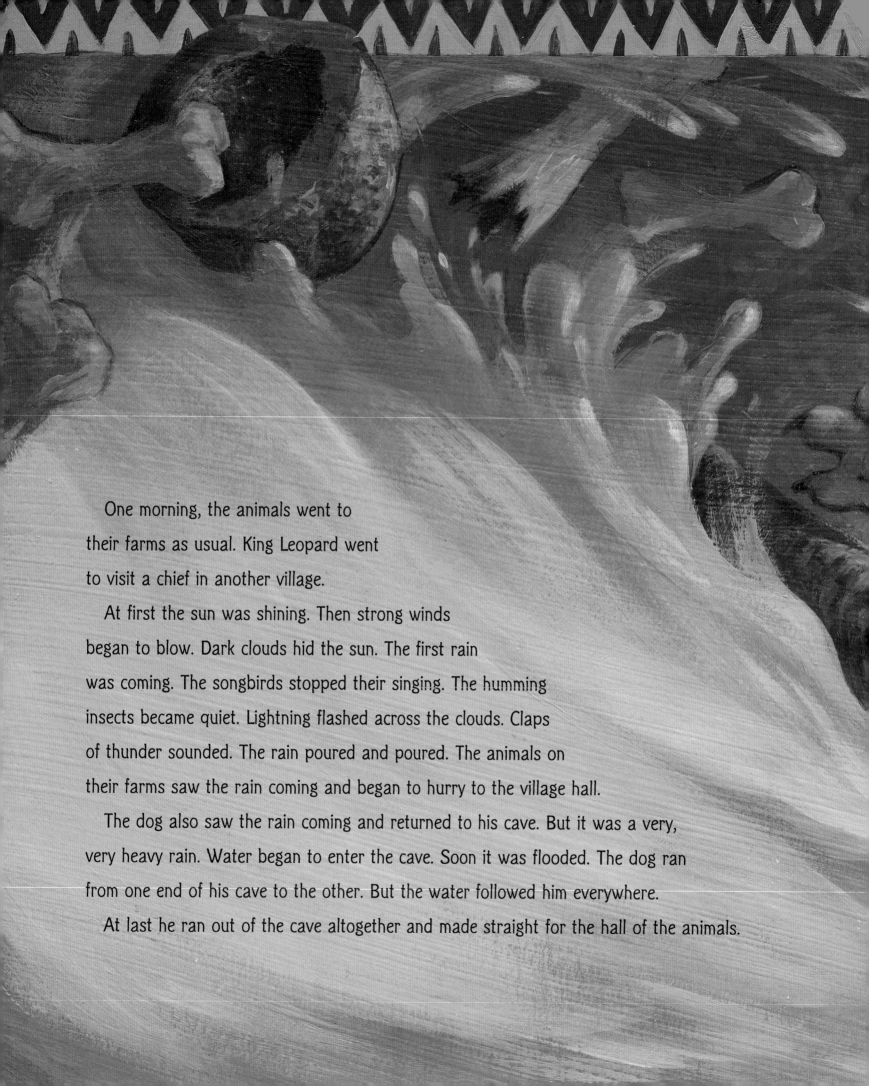

One morning, the animals went to
their farms as usual. King Leopard went
to visit a chief in another village.

At first the sun was shining. Then strong winds
began to blow. Dark clouds hid the sun. The first rain
was coming. The songbirds stopped their singing. The humming
insects became quiet. Lightning flashed across the clouds. Claps
of thunder sounded. The rain poured and poured. The animals on
their farms saw the rain coming and began to hurry to the village hall.

The dog also saw the rain coming and returned to his cave. But it was a very,
very heavy rain. Water began to enter the cave. Soon it was flooded. The dog ran
from one end of his cave to the other. But the water followed him everywhere.

At last he ran out of the cave altogether and made straight for the hall of the animals.

The deer had been the first to arrive. He was surprised to see the dog run up to the hall.

"What do you want here?" asked the deer.

"It is none of your business," replied the dog.

"It is my business," said the deer. "Please stay out. This hall is for those who built it."

Then the dog attacked the deer and bit him with his big, sharp teeth. The deer cried with pain. The dog seized him by the neck and threw him out into the rain, taking his place at the entrance to the hall. The other animals tried to come in one after the other. The dog barked and kept each of them out. They stood together, shivering and crying in the rain. The dog kept barking and showing his teeth.

Then the deer cried out:

"O Leopard, our noble king,

Where are you?

Spotted king of the forest,

Where are you?

Even if you are far away,

Come — hurry home.

The worst has happened to us,

The worst has happened to us:

The house the animals built,

The cruel dog keeps us from it.

The common shelter we built,

The cruel dog keeps us from it.

The worst has happened to us,

The worst has happened to us."

The cry of the deer rang out loud and clear. It was carried by the wind.
King Leopard heard it on his way back from his journey and began to
run toward the village hall. As he got near, he saw the animals, wet and
sheltering under a tree. They were all crying. As he got nearer still, he could
see the dog walking up and down inside the hall.

King Leopard was very angry. "Come out of the hall at once," he said to the dog. The dog barked and rushed at him. They began to fight. The dog bit the leopard and tore his skin with his claws. King Leopard was covered with blood.

The dog went back to the hall. He stood at the door, barking and barking. "Who is next? Who? Who?" he barked.

King Leopard turned to the animals and said, "Let us go in together and drive out the enemy. He is strong, but he is alone. We are many. Together we can drive him out of our house."

But the goat said, "We cannot face him. Look at his strong teeth! He will tear us to pieces!"

"The goat is right," said the animals. "He is too strong for us."

The tortoise stood up and said, "I am sure we are all sorry about what happened to the leopard. But he was foolish to talk to the dog the way he did. It is foolish to annoy such a powerful person as the dog. Let us make peace with him. I don't know what you others think. But I think he should have been our king all along. He is strong; he is handsome. Let us go on our knees and salute him."

"Here, here!" said all the animals. "Hail the dog!"

Tears began to roll down the face of the leopard. His heart was heavy. He loved the animals greatly. But now he knew they were cowards. They had turned their backs on him. So he turned his back on them and went away. Because of his many wounds, he was weak and tired. So he lay down after a while to rest under a tree, far from the village.

The animals saw him go. But they did not care. They were too busy praising their new king, the dog. The tortoise carved a new staff for him. The toad made a new song in his praise:

The dog is great,

The dog is good,

The dog gives us our daily food.

We love his head, we love his jaws.

We love his feet and all his claws.

The dog looked around the circle of animals and asked, "Where is the leopard?"

"We think he has gone away, O king," said the goat.

"Why? He has no right to go away," said the dog. "Nobody has a right to leave our village and its beautiful hall. We must all stay together."

"Indeed!" shouted the animals. "We must stay together! The leopard must return to the village! Our wise king has spoken! It is good to have a wise king!"

The dog then called out the names of six strong animals and said to them, "Go at once and bring back the leopard. If he should refuse to follow you, you must drag him along. If we let him go, others may soon follow his wicked example until there is no one left in our village. That would be a very bad thing, indeed. It is my duty as your king to make sure that we all live together. The leopard is a wicked animal. That is why he wants to go away and live by himself. It is our duty to stop him. Nobody has a right to go away from our village and our beautiful hall."

"Nobody has a right to go away from the village," sang all the animals as the six messengers went to look for the leopard.

They found him resting under the tree beyond the village. Although he was wounded and weak, he still looked like a king. So the six messengers stood at a little distance and spoke to him.

"Our new king, the dog, has ordered you to return to the village," they said.

"He says that no one has a right to leave the village," said the pig.

"Yes, no one has a right to leave our village and its beautiful hall," said the others.

The leopard looked at them with contempt. Then he got up slowly. The six animals fell back. But the leopard did not go toward them. He turned his back on them and began to go away—slowly and painfully. One of the animals picked up a stone and threw it at him. Then all the others immediately picked up stones and began to throw. As they threw, they chanted; "No one has a right to leave our village! No one has a right to leave our village!"

Although some of the stones hit the leopard and hurt him, he did not turn around even once. He continued walking until he no longer heard the noise of the other animals.

The leopard traveled seven days and seven nights. Then he came to the house of the blacksmith. The old man was sitting at his forge. The leopard said to him, "I want the strongest teeth you can make from iron. And I want the most deadly claws you can make from bronze."

The blacksmith asked, "Why do you need such terrible things?" The leopard told his story. Then the blacksmith said, "I do not blame you."

The blacksmith worked a whole day on the teeth, and another full day on the claws. The leopard was pleased with them. He put them on and thanked the blacksmith.

Then he left and went to the house of Thunder. The leopard knocked on the
door, and Thunder roared across the sky.

"I want some of your sound in my voice," said the leopard. "Even a little bit."

"Why do you want my sound in your voice?" asked Thunder. "And why have
you got those terrible teeth and claws?"

The leopard told his story. "I do not blame you," said Thunder. He gave the
sound to the leopard.

"Thank you for the gift," said the leopard. And he began his journey home.

The leopard journeyed for seven days and seven nights and returned to the village of the animals. There he found the animals dancing in a circle around the dog. He stood for a while, watching them with contempt and great anger. They were too busy to notice his presence. He made a deep, terrifying roar. At the same time he sprang into the center of the circle. The animals stopped their song. The dog dropped his staff.

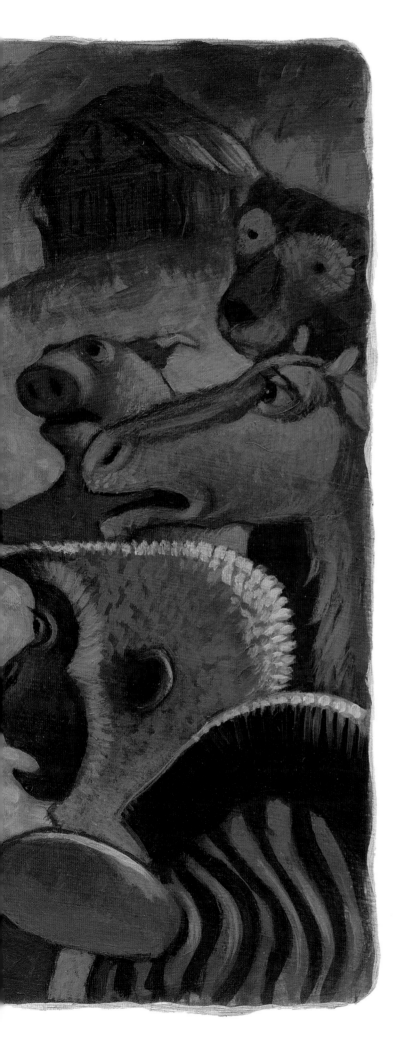

The leopard seized the dog and bit and clawed him without mercy. Then he threw him out of the circle.

All the animals trembled. But they were too afraid to run. The leopard turned to them and said, "You miserable worms. You shameless cowards. I was a kind and gentle king, but you turned against me. From today I shall rule the forest with terror. The life of our village is ended."

"What about our hall?" asked the tortoise in a trembling voice.

"Let everyone take from the hall what he put into it," said the leopard.

The animals began to weep as they had wept long ago in the rain. "Please forgive us, O leopard," they cried.

"Let everyone take from the hall what he put into it," repeated the leopard. "And hurry up!" he thundered.

So the animals pulled their hall apart.
Some carried away the wood, and some took
the roof mats. Others took away doors and
windows. The toad brought his talking drum and
began to beat it to the leopard and to sing:

> *"Alive or dead, the leopard is king.*
> *Beware my friend: Don't twist his tail."*

But the leopard roared like thunder and the
toad dropped his drum. The animals scattered
into the forest.

The dog had already run a long way when the leopard roared. Now he ran faster and faster. His body was covered with blood, and he was very, very weak. He wanted to stop and rest a little. But his fear of the leopard was greater than his weakness. So he staggered and fell and got up and staggered on and on and on.

After many days, the dog came to the house of the hunter.

"Please protect me from the leopard," he cried.

"What will you do for me in return?" asked the hunter.

"I will be your slave," said the dog. "Any day you are hungry for meat, I shall show you the way to the forest. There we can hunt together and kill my fellow animals."

"All right, come in," said the hunter.

Today the animals are no longer friends, but enemies. The strong among them attack and kill the weak. The leopard, full of anger, eats up anyone he can lay his claws on.

And the hunter, led by the dog, goes to the forest from time to time and kills any animals he can find. Perhaps someday the animals will make peace among themselves and live together again. Then, at last, they will be able to keep away the hunter, who is their common enemy.

Text copyright © 1976, 2011 by Chinua Achebe and John Iroaganachi. Illustrations copyright © 2011 by Mary GrandPré. All rights reserved. No part of this book may be reproduced, transmitted, or stored in an information retrieval system in any form or by any means, graphic, electronic, or mechanical, including photocopying, taping, and recording, without prior written permission from the publisher. First U.S. paperback edition 2019. The Library of Congress has cataloged the hardcover edition as follows: Achebe, Chinua. How the leopard got his claws / Chinua Achebe and John Iroaganachi ; illustrated by Mary GrandPré. — 1st U.S. ed. p. cm. Summary: Recounts how the leopard got his claws and teeth and why he rules the forest with terror. ISBN 978-0-7636-4805-3 (hardcover). ISBN 978-1-5362-0949-5 (paperback). [I. Leopard — Fiction. 2. Jungles — Fiction. 3. Allegories.] I. Iroaganachi, John. II. GrandPré, Mary, ill. III. Title. PZ7.A174Ho 2011. [E] — dc22. 2010040344. This book was typeset in Clichee. The illustrations were done in acrylic on gessoed illustration board. The illustrator would like to make the following acknowledgment: "For Tom, my tiger, and Julia, my kitty . . . thank you for your enduring patience." — M. G. Candlewick Press, 99 Dover Street, Somerville, Massachusetts 02144. visit us at www.candlewick.com. Printed in Shenzhen, Guangdong, China. 21 22 23 24 CCP 10 9 8 7 6 5 4 3 2